ONE BEAN

by
Anne Rockwell

pictures by
Megan Halsey

Walker and Company ✺ New York

For Tudy. —A.R.

For Marty, who has always helped me grow. —M.H.

Text copyright © 1998 by Anne Rockwell
Illustrations copyright © 1998 by Megan Halsey

First published in the United States of America in 1998 by Walker Publishing Company, Inc.

Published simultaneously in Canada by Thomas Allen & Son Canada, Limited, Markham, Ontario

Book design by Sophie Ye Chin

Library of Congress Cataloging-in-Publication Data
Rockwell, Anne.
One bean/by Anne Rockwell; pictures by Megan Halsey.
p. cm.
Summary: Describes what happens to a bean as it is soaked, planted, watered, repotted,
and eventually produces pods with more beans inside.
ISBN 0-8027-8648-0 (hc). —ISBN 0-8027-8649-9 (reinforced)
1. Beans—Juvenile literature. 2. Beans—Development—Juvenile literature.
3. Lima bean—Juvenile literature. 4. Lima bean—development—Juvenile literature.
[1. Beans—Development.] I. Halsey, Megan, ill. II. Title.

SB327.R635	1998
635' .653—dc21	97-36249
	CIP
	AC

Printed in Hong Kong
2 4 6 8 10 9 7 5 3 1

I had one bean.
It was dry and smooth and hard.

I put it on a wet paper towel.
I covered it with another wet paper towel.
Soon its skin had turned all wrinkly.

My bean had gotten fatter, too.
I think it got too fat for its skin,
because the skin split.
This meant it was time to plant my bean.

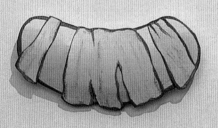

I filled a paper cup
with black potting soil.
Then I laid my fat, wrinkly bean
in the cup and covered it with soil.

I watered it when the soil was dry.
Even though I couldn't see my bean
hidden under the damp, black soil,
I watched for it every day.

Then one day—just like in the story
of Jack and the beanstalk—
something wonderful happened!
A greenish-white stalk poked
up from the soil.
My bean was dangling
from the end of it.

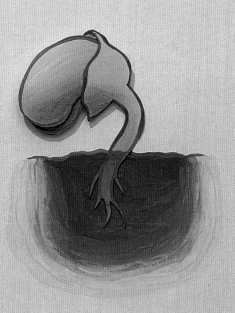

Soon two leaves grew on my bean plant. These were shaped like valentine hearts.

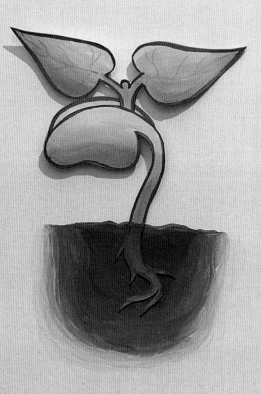

More green, heart-shaped leaves
sprouted.
My bean plant grew bigger and bigger.
It needed a bigger place to live and grow.

I filled a flowerpot with potting soil.
Very gently, very carefully,
I took my one bean with its bright
green leaves and roots spreading
through black, moist soil
out of the paper cup.
I planted it in the flowerpot,
where it could stay.

Sunshine shone on it
and made my bean plant
grow some more.

One day, I saw
lots of little green bumps
on my bean plant.
Those little green bumps were buds.

The buds burst open
and lots of white flowers blossomed
among the green, green leaves.

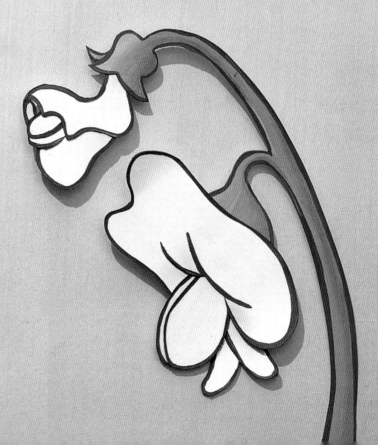

When the white flowers fell off,
tiny, tiny bean pods hung
in their place.
Before long, there were lots of
bean pods growing on my
beautiful bean plant.

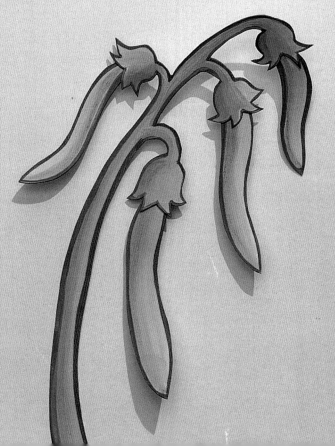

Those tiny bean pods grew bigger.
One day, I picked one.
I split it open and looked inside.
What do you think I saw?
I saw some smooth and shiny beans
shaped just like the one bean
that had started it all!

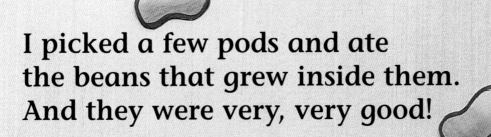

I picked a few pods and ate
the beans that grew inside them.
And they were very, very good!

MORE ACTIVITIES

 Save the seeds you find in the fruits and vegetables you eat. Observe their size, color, and shape. At the end of the week, count how many seeds you saved. Try to remember which fruits and vegetables the seeds came from.

 Make a mosaic of dried beans glued on cardboard. This is fun to do because beans come in many different colors and sizes.

Place dried beans in a paper towel tube and close the ends with tape to make a musical instrument. Use your bean instrument like a maraca and play along to a favorite song.

MORE ABOUT BEANS

What is a bean?

A bean is a seed. Many plants, from dandelions growing in the grass to tall, shady trees, grow from seeds. Some seeds are so tiny you can hardly see them. Some, like nuts and acorns, are big.

Why is a bean a perfect seed to grow?

A bean is a seed called a legume, which grows from the parent plant in an enclosed pod. Legumes are larger than many seeds, so it's easy to see one sprout and grow into a new plant looking just like the plant it came from—as the one in this book does.

Why does the bean in this book look different from the beans you eat for dinner?

From black to white, spotted, speckled, striped, or plain, there are many types of beans—just like there are many types of bean plants. Some bean plants grow tall. Others are low and bushy. The bean in this book is a bush lima bean. Despite the differences, the way a single bean sprouts and grows is always the same.

How do plants grow?

Roots emerge from the seeds underground and absorb water from the soil. Green leaves on the part of the plant above the soil absorb sunlight. The sunlight, water, and soil nourish the plant so it can grow.

What else can you discover from watching seeds turn into plants?

A flower seed will grow into a flower. A pumpkin seed will grow into a pumpkin. An acorn will grow into an oak tree. So try growing many different seeds and see how the plants grow differently—and how they grow alike. It's fun to plant seeds and observe their growth. Now you are a scientist! You are a kind of scientist called a botanist. Botany is the study of plants.

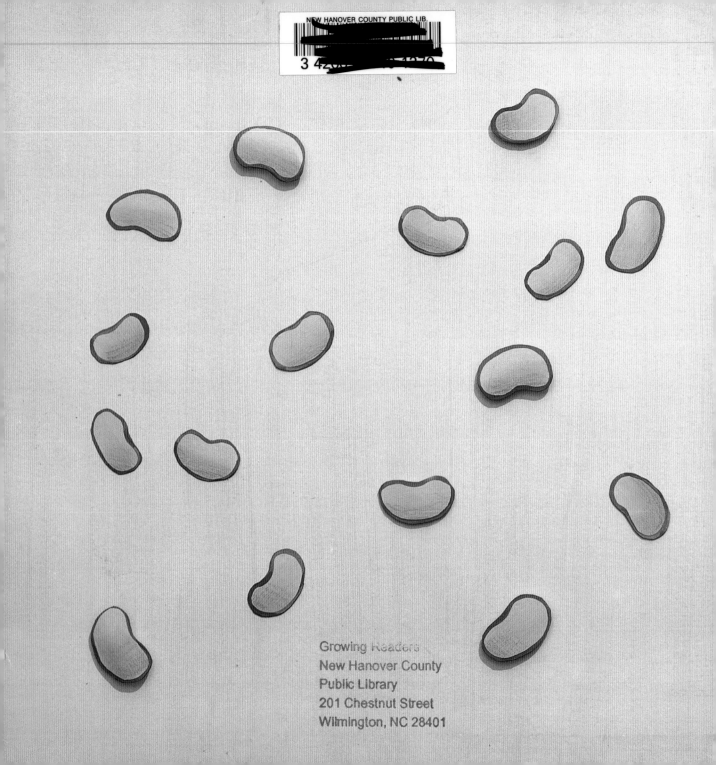